ASTERIX
AND THE GOTHS

TEXT BY GOSCINNY

DRAWINGS BY UDERZO

TRANSLATED BY ANTHEA BELL AND DEREK HOCKRIDGE

*Hodder
Children's
Books*

a division of Hodder Headline plc

Asterix and the Goths

Copyright © Dargaud Editeur 1974, Goscinny-Uderzo
English language text copyright © Brockhampton Press Ltd 1974

First published in Great Britain 1974 (cased) by Hodder Dargaud Ltd
This edition first published 1977 by Knight Books, Hodder Dargaud

This impression: 1996 1997 1998 1999

ISBN 0 340 22171 2

Published by Hodder Dargaud Ltd,
338 Euston Road, London NW1 3BH

Printed in Belgium by Proost International Book Production

The year is 50 BC. Gaul is entirely occupied by the Romans.
Well, not entirely... One small village of indomitable Gauls still
holds out against the invaders. And life is not easy for the
Roman legionaries who garrison the fortified camps of
Totorum, Aquarium, Laudanum and Compendium...

a few of the Gauls

Asterix, the hero of these adventures. A shrewd, cunning little warrior; all perilous missions are immediately entrusted to him. Asterix gets his superhuman strength from the magic potion brewed by the druid Getafix…

Obelix, Asterix's inseparable friend. A menhir delivery-man by trade; addicted to wild boar. Obelix is always ready to drop everything and go off on a new adventure with Asterix – so long as there's wild boar to eat, and plenty of fighting.

Getafix, the venerable village druid. Gathers mistletoe and brews magic potions. His speciality is the potion which gives the drinker superhuman strength. But Getafix also has other recipes up his sleeve…

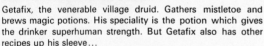

Cacofonix, the bard. Opinion is divided as to his musical gifts. Cacofonix thinks he's a genius. Everyone else thinks he's unspeakable. But so long as he doesn't speak, let alone sing, everybody likes him…

Finally, Vitalstatistix, the chief of the tribe. Majestic, brave and hot-tempered, the old warrior is respected by his men and feared by his enemies. Vitalstatistix himself has only one fear; he is afraid the sky may fall on his head tomorrow. But as he always says, 'Tomorrow never comes.'

IN THE GAULISH VILLAGE WHERE OUR HEROES LIVE, GETAFIX THE DRUID IS BUSY PREPARING FOR HIS VISIT TO THE FOREST OF THE CARNUTES, WHERE THE DRUIDS HOLD THEIR ANNUAL CONFERENCE TO COMPARE NOTES, MEET OLD FRIENDS, AND HOLD A CONTEST TO ELECT THE DRUID OF THE YEAR...

TRALALA 🎵🎵 TRALALA!

WORRIED, 'AFIX. IT'S A LONG 'DANGEROUS AD TO THE REST OF THE RNUTES...

NONSENSE!

LET ME ESCORT YOU GETAFIX!

ASTERIX, YOU KNOW QUITE WELL THAT NON-DRUIDS AREN'T ALLOWED AT THE CONFERENCE!

I'LL GO TO THE EDGE OF THE FOREST WITH YOU AND WAIT FOR YOU THERE...

OH, VERY WELL. IF YOU INSIST.

AN I COME TOO? NHIRS ARE OUT OF EASON AT THE MOMENT.

I WILL NOW SING A SONG OF FAREWELL!

OH NO, YOU WON'T! OH NO, YOU WON'T! OH NO, YOU WON'T!

POP! POP! POP!

FAR AWAY, ON THE EASTERN FRONTIER OF GAUL, TWO LEGIONARIES ARE ON GUARD DUTY...

When I count three!

?

YOU ARE NOW LEAVING THE ROMAN EMPIRE

HOLD IT! I THOUGHT I HEARD SOMEONE SPEAKING GOTHIC OVER THERE!

BLAM!

YOU'RE IMAGINING THINGS, ARTERIOSCLEROSUS!

BUT GASTROENTERITUS, I COULD HAVE SWORN...!

THE BARBARIAN VISIGOTHS, OSTROGOTHS, OR ANY OTHER GOTHS WOULD NEVER DARE TO SULLY ROMAN TERRITORY WITH THEIR DIRTY FEET, BY JUPITER!

Three! Jump to it!

!

!?

YOU ARE NOW LEAVING THE ROMAN EMPIRE

BANG!

PA

VLAN!

WHAT DID I JUST SAY?

ERRARE HUMANUM EST...

Well done, Tartaric, Atmospheric, Prehistoric and Esoteric! And now to the Forest of the Carnutes!

Long live our chief Choleric!!!

...E THESE SERIOUS FRONTIER ...ENTS ARE TAKING PLACE, OUR ...NDS ARE ON THEIR WAY TO ... FOREST OF THE CARNUTES...

WE'LL SOON BE THERE. YOU SEE, IT WAS QUITE AN UNEVENTFUL JOURNEY!

BETTER SAFE THAN SORRY...

I'M A BIT PECKISH...

OH! WHAT A PLEASANT SURPRISE!

A WILD BOAR?!

FRIENDS, LET ME INTRODUCE YOU TO MY OLD FRIEND AND COLLEAGUE, THE BRITISH DRUID VALUADDETAX!

OH, I SAY! DELIGHTED, I'M SURE!

...ME ALONG, VALUADDETAX! ...GOING TO AMAZE YOU WITH ...Y DRUIDICAL PROWESS!

WAIT TILL YOU SEE MINE, OLD BOY!

HALT! WHO GOES THERE?

A ROMAN PATROL!

SHALL WE GET THEM?

NO, NO, OBELIX. WHILE THE CONFERENCE IS ON THERE'S A TRUCE WITH THE ROMANS.

...LET US PASS, ...ECURION. WE ARE ...RUIDS GOING TO THE ...OREST OF THE CARNUTES.

THAT'S YOUR STORY. JUST PROVE IT!

PROVE THAT WE'RE REAL DRUIDS? NOTHING SIMPLER! WE'LL SHOW YOU OUR MAGIC POWERS...

LET ME, GETAFIX! BE A SPORT!

OH, VERY WELL...

I NEED A VOLUNTEER.

LEGIONARY CADAVERUS! YOU'RE VOLUNTEERING!

?

WOULD YOU EAT THESE HERBS, PLEASE?

SCRUNCH!

SCRUNCH!

WELL, WHERE'S THIS 'ERE MAGIC, THEN?

JUST ASK YOUR LEGIONARY TO SAY SOMETHING...

SAY SOMETHING!

HEE-HAW!

HA! HA! HE CAN'T SPEAK ANY MORE, HE CAN ONLY BRAY HO! HO! HO!

IT HASN'T MADE THAT MUCH DIFFERENCE!

?

HA! HA! HI! HI! HI! HO! HO!

ALL RIGHT, YOU CAN PASS. YOU'RE REAL DRUIDS. WE'RE CHECKING UP BECAUSE A HORDE OF GOTHS HAS CROSSED THE FRONTIER. THEY'VE BEEN SEEN IN THIS AREA.

HEE-HAW!

SILENCE IN THE RANKS! FORWARD MARCH!

IT'S A JOLLY GOOD JOB WE DID COME WITH YOU, GETAFIX, WITH ALL THESE BARBARIANS PROWLING AROUND!

HUH! WARS BETWEEN BARBARIANS AND ROMANS ARE NO CONCERN OF OURS...

FOREST OF THE CARNUTES

NON-DRUIDS KEEP OUT

AH, WE'RE THERE!

IGHT, WE'LL WAIT HERE NTIL THE CONFERENCE S OVER.

VERY WELL

GOOD LUCK IN THE COMPETITION!

LET'S MAKE OURSELVES COMFORTABLE.

I WONDER WHAT THE BARBARIANS ARE DOING AROUND HERE...

THIS IS A GOOD SPOT... PLENTY OF WILD BOAR ABOUT!

D NOT FAR AWAY...

Well men, you know why we're here...

Our mission is to capture the best Gaulish druid. We'll take him back across the border, and then, with the help of his magic, we'll plan the invasion of Gaul and Rome...

To the greater glory of the Visigoths, the Ostrogoths, and any other sort of Goths!

Long live Choleric, our chief!

Silence! Let's eavesdrop on the conference and capture the druid who wins first prize!

DO YOU KNOW, VALUADDETAX, I FEEL SURE I'M GOING TO WIN FIRST PRIZE AND BE ELECTED DRUID OF THE YEAR!

FIRST CANDIDATE... DRUID BOTANIX!

JUST A FEW DROPS OF POTION ON THE GROUND...

CLAP! CLAP! CLAP! ...AND THERE YOU HAVE MAGNIFICENT OUT-OF-SEASON FLOWERS!

CLAP! CLAP!

QUITE CHARMING!

CLAP! CLAP! CLAP! HOW DELIGHTFUL...

CLAP! CLAP!

SHUT UP, YOU IDIOT!

CLAP! CLAP! CLAP!

WHAT'S UP? I CAN LIKE FLOWERS EVEN IF I AM A BARBARIAN, CAN'T I?

HNNMFF!

CANDIDATE NUMBER TWO: DRUID PREFIX!

I JUST THROW SOME POWDER IN THE AIR...

...AND I MAKE IT RAIN!

NOT BAD!

THE WEATHER'S ALL TOPSY-TURVY THESE DAYS!

ATISHOO!

DRUID SUFFIX!

PARP!

I HAVE INVENTED A METHOD OF MAKING POWDERED SOUP SO THAT IT CAN BE CARRIED ABOUT IN LITTLE PACKETS, MUCH LESS BOTHER THAN A CAULDRON!

JT TO MAKE IT TO SOUP YOU ILL NEED A AULDRON...

I'VE THOUGHT OF EVERYTHING, O VENERABLE CHIEF DRUID...

I'VE INVENTED A METHOD OF MAKING POWDERED CAULDRONS TOO!

WELL DONE!

HOW INGENIOUS!

VERY CLEVER!

THE COMPETITION'S BEGUN. THEY SEEM TO BE ENJOYING THEMSELVES!

YOU MARK MY WORDS, OBELIX! I'M CERTAIN OUR DRUID WILL WIN FIRST PRIZE WITH HIS MAGIC POTION.

NON-DRUIDS KEEP OUT

BRAVO!

CLAP! CLAP! CLAP!

11

AND NOW WE COME TO THE NEXT CANDIDATE, VALUADDETAX!

I HAVE BREWED A POTION WHICH MAKES YOU IMMUNE TO PAIN! JUST WATCH THIS...

GLUG! GLUG! GLUG!

..AND NOW I CAN TAKE CHIPS OUT OF BOILING OIL WITH MY BARE HANDS!!

VERY PRACTICAL!

GREAT

CLAP! CLAP!

CLAP! CLAP! CLAP! CLAP!

CLAP!

AND NOW OUR LAST CANDIDATE... DRUID GETAFIX!

I SHOULD LIKE TO DEMONSTRATE MY POTION WHICH GIVES A MAN SUPERHUMAN STRENGTH!

I NEED THE HELP OF A FEEBLE DRUID!

I'M A FEEBLE DRUID...

DRINK THIS, AND THEN GO AND UPROOT AN OAK TREE, FEEBLE DRUID!

THIS ONE?

EEEEEK! OOOOOH!

CRAAAACK!

ARE YOU OUT YOUR MIND?

HEY, CAN'T YOU LET US CUT MISTLETOE IN PEACE?!!

I HAD ALREADY HEARD ABOUT YOUR POTION, GETAFIX, BUT IT'S EVEN MORE IMPRESSIVE THAN I'D BEEN LED TO BELIEVE!

CAN I GO NOW?

HURRAH! HE'S THE WINNER!

That's the one we want!

ECLARE GETAFIX DRUID OF ? YEAR, AND HAVE GREAT EASURE IN PRESENTING IM WITH THE GOLDEN MENHIR!

WORDS FAIL ME!

BRAVO! HURRAY!

CONGRATULATIONS!

IT WAS SO UNEXPECTED...

HE CONFERENCE IS OVER, ETAFIX. WE CAN SET OFF GETHER, IF YOU LIKE!

WITH PLEASURE, VALUADDETAX. I'LL JUST GO AND GET MY THINGS.

I'M THE GREATEST! I'M THE GREATEST! I'M THE GREATEST!

Ready?

Ready!

WHAT THE...

!

Now let's get out of here!!!

HMMMM HMMMMM!

EANWHILE...

WHERE ON EARTH IS GETAFIX?

THE CONFERENCE IS OVER, BUT THERE'S NO SIGN OF GETAFIX ANYWHERE...

DID YOU HEAR? IT SEEMS THAT HE WON THE COMPETITION!

DRUIDS

I'M WORRIED, OBELIX... LETS GO AND FIND HIM!

13

OH, THERE YOU ARE, YOU CHAPS! I'M FRIGHTFULLY WORRIED. GETAFIX HAS DISAPPEARED!

HE WENT THAT WAY...

LET'S GO AND SEE!

LOOK AT THIS!

THAT'S A VISIGOTH HELMET! WHAT A TERRIBLE CALAMITY! WE'LL NEVER SEE OUR FRIEND AGAIN!

OH YES, WE WILL! WE'LL SNATCH HIM FROM THE CLUTCHES OF THE BARBARIANS!

I THOUGHT THEY WERE VISIGOTHS

GOOD SHOW! I'M COMING WITH YOU!

THANK YOU, VALUADDETAX, BUT OBELIX AND I WILL MANAGE ON OUR OWN.

JUST SHOW ME THE CAULDRON WHERE OUR DRUID MADE HIS MAGIC POTION!

IT'S THAT ONE OVER THERE!

GLUG! GLUG! GLUG!

GOOD LUCK, FRIENDS!

WHERE ARE WE OFF TO NOW?

TO THE BORDER! EAST, TO THE COUNTRY OF THE VISIGOTHS!

SO THE VISIGOTHS ARE GOTHS FROM THE EAST?

NO, THE VISIGOTHS ARE GOTHS FROM THE WEST. THE GOTHS FROM THE EAST ARE OSTRO-GOTHS, BUT IN RELATION TO US, THE GOTHS FROM THE WEST LIVE IN THE EAST. DO YOU SEE?

NO!

THINGS ARE GETTING COMPLICATED. NOT ONLY HAVE WE LOST TIME, BUT THE ROMANS WILL BE AFTER US NOW!

AND IN A NEARBY ROMAN CAMP, IN THE TENT OF GENERAL CANTANKERUS...

BY JUPITER! IT SEEMS INCREDIBLE! BARBARIANS WANDERING ABOUT ON ROMAN TERRITORY AND GETTING AWAY WITH IT! IF JULIUS CAESAR HEARS OF THIS, WE'LL ALL BE SERVED UP IN THE CIRCUS AS THE LIONS' DINNER!

AYE, GENERAL! THE PATROL IS BACK!

SEND THE LEADER IN!

AYE, GENERAL! WE FOUND THE HORDE OF BARBARIANS, BUT WE WERE DEFEATED.

TELL ME WHAT THIS HORDE WAS LIKE.

THERE WAS A FAT ONE AND A LITTLE ONE!

I'LL DRAW YOU A PICTURE...

GET COPIES OF THIS PICTURE MADE AND HAVE THEM SENT TO EVERY CAMP IN THE AREA!

WE'VE GOT TO LAY HANDS ON THOSE TWO GOTHS!

HANDS WILL BE LAID ON THEM ALL RIGHT, AND IT WON'T TAKE LONG, I CAN PROMISE YOU THAT!

RUNNERS SET OFF IN ALL DIRECTIONS...

... AND SOON AFTERWARDS...

SOMEONE'S COMING!

LET'S CLIMB THIS TREE!

A ROMAN LEGIONARY!

HOW DO YOU KNOW THAT?

LET'S CAPTURE HIM AND FIND OUT WHY HE'S RUNNING

RIGHT!

CRUNCH

?!? IT'S A PICTURE OF US!!!

HO, HO! ISN'T IT GOOD!

THERE'S SOMETHING WRITTEN UNDERNEATH, AND THAT'S NOT SO GOOD. "WANTED, DEAD OR ALIVE, TWO GOTHS, LARGE REWARD."

THOSE IDIOTS WILL BE AFTER US NOW, INSTEAD OF LOOKING FOR THE BARBARIANS!

YES, THEY'LL BE CHASING GAULS FROM THE WEST INSTEAD OF GOTHS FROM THE EAST. THEY'RE ALL UP THE POLE

SURE ENOUGH, TOTAL DISORDER REIGNS IN THE FOREST. THE ROMANS CAN'T SEE THE WOOD FOR THE TREES, AND THE ONLY ONES WHO ARE NOT WORRIED ARE THE BARBARIANS...

Ours not to reason why!

AS SOON AS THE ROMANS KNOW THAT THE GOTHS THEY ARE LOOKING FOR ARE DISGUISED AS ROMANS, THERE IS COMPLETE CHAOS... THE ROMANS GO ABOUT CAPTURING ONE ANOTHER...

I'M TAKING YOU IN, GOTH!

YOU OFF YOUR HEAD OR SOMETHING?

I'M A ROMAN! I'M A ROMAN! I'M A ROMAN!

GOT YOU, YOU BARBARIAN!

THE UNHAPPY GENERAL CANTANKER IS NEARLY OUT OF HIS MIND...

THEY'RE ALL QUITE THICK, AND I'M THEIR LEADER! (SOB! SOB!)

BUT SOME PEOPLE ARE MAKING THE MOST OF THE SITUATION, FOR INSTANCE, ASTERIX AND OBELIX, WHO HAVE PUT THEIR OWN CLOTHES ON AGAIN...

...AND THE GOTHS, THE ROOT OF ALL THE TROUBLE, WHO ARE PROCEEDING UNEVENTFULLY TOWARDS THEIR OWN COUNTRY OF GERMANIA.

Watch out! The frontier's ahead. We've got to cross it !

A HEAVY RESPONSIBILITY WEIGHS ON THOSE WHO GUARD THE FRONTIER AGAINST FOREIGN INVADERS...

GAUL
RUMAN
EMPIRE

Germania

Hey!

HMMM?

BONG

Victory is ours! We'll be given a hero's welcome by our own people !

Anything to declare ?

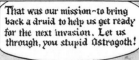

HEY!

GAUL
ROMAN
EMPIRE

HMMM?

BANG!

HOW TEDIOUS THESE BORDER FORMALITIES CAN BE!

SIR! SIR! IT'S HAPPENED! THIS TIME IT'S A REAL INVASION!!!

?!?!

AN INVASION?! WHERE? WHERE?

TWO GAULS, CROSSING THE BORDER INTO GERMANIA!

NO! NO! AN INVASION IS WHEN PEOPLE CROSS THE BORDER INTO OUR COUNTRY, NOT THE OTHER WAY ROUND!

BUT SIR, YOU SAID...

AND YOU WILL DO FOUR DAYS INSIDE, THAT'LL TEACH YOU TO TRY AND BE CLEVER!!!

WELL, I ASK YOU

MEANWHILE, THE GOTHS HAVE MANAGED TO GET OVER THEIR OWN ADMINISTRATIVE DIFFICULTIES...

O great chief Metric, we have brought you the champion druid, whose magic will help us conquer Gaul and the whole of the Roman Empire!

Well done! Have him put in the cage. We'll interrogate him later!

WATCH OUT! SOMEONE'S COMING

Who are you?

I DON'T UNDERSTAND GOTHIC, BUT I THINK HE'S ASKING WHO WE ARE...

AVE, BY JUPITER! I'M LEGIONARY OBELUS AND MY FRIEND IS LEGIONARY ASTERUS!

!

CHCHCHCHCHCHCH!

If I'm not much mistaken, these are Romans coming to invade us. Let's get them!

PAFF!

BOUM!

BIMK!

LET'S GO AND HIDE IN THE UNDERGROWTH, OBELIX. THERE ARE ONE OR TWO THINGS I MUST EXPLAIN...

WE DON'T HAVE TO PRETEND TO BE ROMANS ANY MORE, OBELIX. WE'D BE BETTER OFF DISGUISED AS GOTHS...

WHY?

ARE YOU READY, OBELIX? HERE'S YOUR SIZE COMING!

Hey!

ONE HOUR LATER...

AT LAST! I THOUGHT THIS ONE WAS NEVER GOING TO TURN UP!

OUCH!

WHAM!

BIFF!

LET'S PUT THE GOTHIC HELMETS OVER OUR GAULISH ONES. THAT'LL HELP US LOOK MORE CONVINCING!

RIGHT!

JUST REMEMBER, WE DON'T KNOW THEIR LANGUAGE, SO ON NO ACCOUNT SPEAK TO ANY GOTHS!

WE CAN BASH THEM THOUGH, CAN'T WE?!

MEANWHILE...

O Metric, Rhetoric the interpreter is here!

Show him in!

If this druid refuses my demands, I shall be very angry, Rhetoric. I shall have the druid killed, and you along with him. Understand?

Y...yes!

Ask him if he's prepared to use his magic powers in our cause...

ARE YOU PREPARED TO USE YOUR MAGIC POWERS IN OUR CAUSE?

NEVER!

Perhaps...

Tell him to say yes or no!

YES OR NO?

NO!

YES!

Excellent! When will he show us his magic?

In a week's time, at the full moon

PHEW! THAT GIVES ME A BREATHING SPACE!

HOW ARE WE GOING TO FIND OUR DRUID, ASTERIX?

I'M NOT SURE YET... QUICK, LET'S HIDE! THERE ARE SOME SOLDIERS COMING!

Left! Right! Left! Right!

Left, Right! Left, Right!

O-oh grand old Alaric, he had ten thousand men...♪ ♫ ♫

LET'S FOLLOW THOSE MEN! SOMETHING TELLS ME WE'LL FIND OUR DRUID IF WE CAN GET TO THEIR CHIEF.

Left! Right! Left! Right!

He marched them up to the gates of Rome, and...♪ ♫

IT'S A LONG WAY TO AQUARIUM ♪ ♫

SSH! OBELIX!

WE'RE COMING TO A TOWN. LET'S SLIP AWAY!

Hey! You there!

No breaking ranks! Keep in step! You're both on a charge! Left! Right! Left! Right!

WHAT'S HE SAYING?

KEEP QUIET, OBELIX OURS NOT TO REASON WHY...

WE'LL GET AWAY TONIGHT. TILL THEN, WE MUSTN'T MAKE OURSELVES CONSPICUOUS WE DON'T WANT THEM NOTICING WE'RE GAULS!

Left! Right! Left! Right!

...TERIX AND OBELIX ARE
...T THE ONLY ONES WITH
...CAPE IN MIND, FOR IN
...OTHER PART OF THE TOWN...

I'LL GO TO GAUL, WITH MY KNOWLEDGE OF MODERN LANGUAGES I'LL BE ABLE TO GET A JOB THERE...

Halt! Who goes there?

THE PATROL!

Well, if it isn't Rhetoric the interpreter! And where might you be off to at this time of night?

Well, I...er... the fact is... well, it was like this, you see...

No, I don't! It's the guardroom for you! You can explain yourself tomorrow!

No, No! You're making a big mistake! I've got friends in high places!!!

...M DONE FOR! THE
...IEF WILL NEVER
...ORGIVE ME FOR
...CEIVING HIM ABOUT
...AT THAT PIG-HEADED
...DRUID SAID...

MEANWHILE...

GOT IT? NO FIGHTING, AND NO TALKING TO ANY GOTHS.

RIGHT!

EEEK! THATS TORN IT!

Hullo, hullo, hullo! Who have we here? You're for the guardroom too!

YOU DO SPEAK GAULISH!

NO! NO! IT'S ALL A MISTAKE! I DON'T SPEAK GAULISH! NOT A WORD OF GAULISH! I DON'T HAVE ANY GIFT FOR LANGUAGES!

TELL US WHERE OUR DRUID GETAFIX IS.

AND I WON'T SAY A WORD EITHER, SO THERE!

CARRY ON, OBELIX!

GOODY, GOODY!

...ERY FAST) THE DRUID IS BEING ...EPT PRISONER BY OUR CHIEF ...ETRIC. HE HAS TO PROVE HE ...AN WORK MAGIC AT THE TIME ... THE NEW MOON, OR HE'LL BE EXECUTED...

...I'LL GIVE YOU THE ADDRESS, BUT LET ME GO! I'M IN DANGER OF BEING EXECUTED TOO!

TALKATIVE, ISN'T HE, WHEN HE FEELS LIKE IT...

LET'S GET BACK TO THE TOWN!

I ORDER YOU TO LET ME GO!

WE'LL LET YOU GO WHEN WE FIND OUR DRUID, AND NOT BEFORE!

PATROLS EVERYWHERE! THEY'VE DISCOVERED THAT WE'VE GONE!

OVER HERE! THIS WAY! I'VE CAUGHT TWO GAULISH SPIES!

QUICK, OBELIX! COME ON!

THERE! OVER THERE! GET THEM!

I WONDER WHAT THAT SAYS?

THIS IS NO TIME TO WORRY ABOUT FOREIGN ROAD SIGNS!

NO THROUGH ROAD

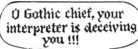

BOOHOOHOO.

NO POINT IN OUR DISGUISES NOW...

WE'LL TALK WHEN THE INTERPRETER'S GONE TO SLEEP.

BONG!

HE'S GONE TO SLEEP WE CAN TALK.

!?

WE HAVE TO ESCAPE AT ONCE AND GET BACK TO GAUL!

YES, BUT BEFORE LEAVING THE COUNTRY, WE MUST DISCOURAGE THE GOTHS FROM INVADING US...AND MAKE SURE THEY STAY DISCOURAGED!

HOWEVER ARE YOU GOING TO MANAGE THAT?

WE'LL SPREAD A BIT OF DISORDER AND CONFUSION!

AND THIS COWARDLY, GREEDY, TWO-FACED INTERPRETER WILL COME IN USEFUL. HE'S ABSOLUTELY IDEAL FOR OUR PURPOSES... NOW THEN, THIS IS MY PLAN...

HA HA HA! HO! HO!

That's funny! The prisoners are laughing ...

They wouldn't be feeling so cheerful if they knew the tortur~ that are in store for them!

HAHAHA HAHA! HA! HA!

HA! HA! HEE! HEE! HEE! HO! HO!

HAHAHA HAHA! HA! HA!

HEE! HEE! HEE! HO! HO! HO! HA! HA! HA!

It really is a very happy prison!

WAKE HIM UP.

RIGHT!

COME ON LAZYBONES! GET UP! GET UP!

OOOOOOH! SO IT WASN'T ALL A NIGHTMARE!

ONDEMNED TO DEATH! ST WHEN I WAS GOING TO ET MARRIED AND HAVE OTS OF LITTLE BARBARIANS...

LISTEN, WE'RE SORRY WE GOT YOU INTO THIS SPOT...

WHAT GOOD IS THAT? IT WON'T KEEP ME FROM THE CRUEL VENGEANCE OF METRIC!

AH, BUT IT WILL! I'M GOING TO MAKE YOU A PRESENT OF SOME OF MY MAGIC. YOU'LL BE THE STRONGEST OF ALL THE GOTHS. NO ONE WILL BE ABLE TO STAND UP TO YOU!

IS... IS HE OKING?

NOT AT ALL!

QUICK! QUICK! LET'S HAVE A LOOK AT THIS MAGIC!

I NEED CERTAIN INGREDIENTS...

CALL THE GUARD, OBELIX!

RIGHT.

YOOHOO! ANYONE THERE?

?!

RAAASH!

Go and ask Metric's permission for us to have a last bowl of Gaulish soup... here's the list of ingredients we need

?!

FIRE BURN AND CAULDRON BUBBLE...

ASTERIX, YOU'D BETTER HAVE SOME TOO. I THINK YOU'RE GOING TO NEED IT.

WHAT ABOUT ME?

...MANY TIMES DO I HAVE TO TELL YOU YOU HAVEN'T ...ED ANY EVER SINCE YOU FELL INTO A CAULDRON OF POTION WHEN YOU WERE A BABY? YOU ...Y PERFECTLY WELL THAT IT HAD A ...MANENT EFFECT ...N YOU!

IT'S NOT FAIR! IT'S JUST NOT FAIR!

IT'S READY. DRINK UP.

SLORP! SLURP!

IT HASN'T HAD ANY EFFECT ON ME...

YOU THINK NOT? TRY YOUR STRENGTH ON THAT DOOR...

GLUG GLUG!

CRAAAASH!

WILL-YOU-KINDLY-LEAVE-THAT-DOOR-ALONE!!!

YOOHOOOOO! I'M STRONG! I'M POWERFUL! I'M GOING TO SMASH METRIC! I'M GOING TO CONQUER THE VISIGOTHS AND THE ROMANS AND THE GAULS!

WAIT UNTIL IT'S TIME FOR OUR EXECUTION BEFORE YOU ACT. THAT WILL BE GOOD PUBLICITY!

YES, THAT'S A VERY GOOD IDEA!

I'LL BE OVERLORD OF ALL THE GOTHS! EMPEROR OF THE WORLD!

IT'S WORKING!

Now, everyone listen to me! I've got some of the Gaulish druid's magic powers! I'm your new chief, Rhetoric I!

That's the stuff! Down with Metric!

Hurrah! Long live Rhetoric I!

PLATCH!

CLAP! CLAP! CLAP!

Just a minute! I'm the chief around here!

Throw this poor fish into the dungeons! It's time you were going, Metric

SOON AFTERWARDS, IN THE PALACE...

COME ALONG IN, FRIENDS, COME ALONG IN. I WAS JUST PLANNING THE PROGRAMME FOR METRIC'S TORTURE TOMORROW.

What were we saying?

Well, and then we could put him in a double saucepan and stir over a slow flame...

SORRY TO INTERRUPT YOU, RHETORIC, BUT WE HAVE A FAVOUR TO ASK YOU...

YES? ANYTHING YOU LIKE, MY DEAR ASTERIX!

WE WANT TO VISIT METRIC IN HIS DUNGEON, TO CROW OVER HIM...

AN EXCELLENT IDEA! OFF YOU GO! HAVE A NICE TIME!

IT'S STILL WORKING!

When these Gauls have served their purpose I'll have to get rid of them...

I've got something special for them: a pressure cooker. It can cook a person in a couple of minutes, and it whistles when he's done!

Hee, hee! You can't stop progress!

...ERIX, GETAFIX AND OBELIX MAKE THEIR WAY ...K TO THE DUNGEON FOR A WORD WITH ...TRIC...

Metric, would you like to get your revenge on Rhetoric and return to power?

?

HE SAYS YES!

I GOT THE GENERAL IDEA!

...re a swig of this magic ...tion... then you'll be as ...ong as Rhetoric. The way ...a use your strength is up to you...

GLUG! GLUG!

CLINNNK!

HE'S GOT A FREE HAND NOW!

CRAAAAASH!

Here we go again! They ought to replace that door by a curtain!

Raise the alarm! The prisoner's escaping !!!

So what?

POC!

HE'S GOT A FREE HAND! HA!HA!HA! THAT'S A GOOD ONE, THAT IS! I'VE ONLY JUST GOT IT. HO!HO!HO!

ANOTHER CANDIDATE!

Drink this!

GLUG! GLUG!

AND OUR THREE GAULS CARRY ON WITH THEIR CAMPAIGN TO DISTURB THE PEACE...

Drink this!

GLUG! GLUG!

Drink this!

GLUG! GLUG!

Drink this!

GLUG! GLUG!

Drink this!

GLUG! GLUG!

Drink this!

GLUG! GLUG!

...WHILE EVERY ONE OF THEIR PATIENTS, INVINCIBLY STRONG, AND SPURRED ON BY THE REMARKS OF OUR FRIENDS, SETS OUT TO RECRUIT AN ARMY...

TCHOC!

And that makes 250 - a company

FIGHTING STARTS BETWEEN THE DIFFERENT FACTIONS...

Up with Electric!

Rhetoric for chief!

Metric for chief!

PAF!

PING!

Euphoric for chief!

THE GOURD OF POTION IS EMPTY...

BUT WHAT WILL HAPPEN WHEN THE GOTHS FIND THE EFFECTS OF THE POTION WEARING OFF?

NOTHING. THEY'LL ALL BE IN THE SAME BOAT. BEING MORE OR LESS EQUAL, THEY'LL GO ON FIGHTING EACH OTHER FOR CENTURIES... AND THEY WON'T STOP TO THINK ABOUT INVADING THEIR NEIGHBOURS.

WELL, NOW THAT OUR PEACE-MAKING MISSION IS ACCOMPLISHED, ALL WE HAVE TO DO IS GO HOME TO GAUL!

OOH, YES! I CAN'T WAIT TO TASTE WILD BOAR THE WAY MOTHER MADE IT!

Metric

Rhetoric

THE ASTERIXIAN WARS
A Tangled Web . . .

The ruse employed by Asterix, Getafix and Obelix succeeded beyond their wildest dreams. After drinking the druid's magic potion, the Goths fought each other tooth and nail. Here is a brief summary to help you follow the history of these famous wars.

The favourite and devastating weapon of the combatants.

Diagram indicating the course of events.

The first victory is won outright by Rhetoric, who, having surprised Metric by an outflanking movement, lets him have it – bonk! – and inflicts a crushing defeat on him. This defeat, however, is only temporary . . .

...oric has no time to celebrate his victory, for, having ...pleted his outflanking movement, he is taken in the ... by his own ally, Lyric. Lyric instantly proclaims ...elf supreme chief of all the Goths, much to the ...sement of the other chiefs . . . .

Who turn out to be right, for Lyric's brother-in-law Satiric lays an ambush for him, pretending to invite him to a family reunion and Lyric falls into the trap. It was upon this occasion that the proposition that blood is thicker than water was first put to the test . . .

Rhetoric goes after Lyric, with the avowed intention of "bashing him up" (archaic), but his rearguard is surprised by Metric's vanguard. Bonk! This manoeuvre is known as the Metric System.

...eral Electric manages to surprise Euphoric meditating ...the conduct of his next few campaigns. Euphoric's ...ale is distinctly lowered, but he has the last word, ...his famous remark, "I'll short-circuit him yet"

While Electric proclaims himself supreme chief of the Goths, to the amusement of all and sundry, it is the turn of Metric's rearguard to be surprised by Rhetoric's vanguard. Bonk! "This is bad for my system," is the comment of the exasperated Metric.

In fact, it is so bad for his system that he allows himself to be surprised by Euphoric. The battle is short and sharp. Euphoric, a wily politician, instantly proclaims himself supreme chief of the Goths. The other supreme chiefs are in fits . . .

...horic, much annoyed, sets up camp and decides to ... He is surprised by Eccentric, who in his turn is ...ked by Lyric, subsequently to be defeated by ...ric. Electric is destined to be betrayed by Satiric, will be beaten by Rhetoric.

Going round a corner, Rhetoric's vanguard bumps into Metric's vanguard. Bonk! Bonk! This battle is famous in the Asterixian wars as the "Battle of the Two Losers" And so the war goes on . . .

MEANWHILE, OUR THREE FRIENDS ARE APPROACHING THE FRONTIER OF GAUL, WITH THEIR MINDS AT REST...

THERE'S THE FRONTIER!

I CAN SMELL THE BOARS ALREADY!

?!

GAUL ROMAN EMPIRE

HALT! WHO GOES THERE?

I MUST SAY, IT'S NICE...

GAUL ROMAN EMPIRE

German

PAFF!

...TO GET HOME...

GAUL ROMAN EMPIRE

Germania

...AND I CAN'T WAIT TO SEE OUR OWN VILLAGE AGAIN!

GAUL ROMAN EMPIRE

?

G R E N

SIR! SIR! THERE'S JUST BEEN AN INVASION!

!?!

GOTHS?

NO, GAULS.

CLAC!

GAULS INVADING GAUL? WONDERFUL! AS HELPFUL AS EVER, I SEE! I SUPPOSE YOU STILL THINK I'M A FOOL...?

POF! POF! POF!

IT'S VIII DAYS CONFINED TO BARRACKS FOR YOU, IV OF THEM ON FATIGUES!!!

BUT, SIR...

AND FINALLY, HAVING CROSSED GAUL FROM EAST TO WEST...

OUR VILLAGE!

PRINTED IN BELGIUM BY
proost
INTERNATIONAL BOOK PRODUCTION